The Girl Who Married A Ghost

and other tales from Nigeria

Ifeoma Onyefulu

Illustrated by Julia Cairns

F

FRANCES LINCOLN
CHILDREN'S BOOKS

Contents

Introduction

When we were children, in our village in Eastern Nigeria, I and my brothers and sister were told lots of stories by our mother, grandparents, aunts and uncles, and sometimes family friends. We were catapulted from our familiar surroundings into strange worlds where spirits ruled, and where animals could talk and reason. A world where Tortoise (the most popular character) outwitted even his friends to save his own skin. He was a true villain, but we loved his tricks.

The stories were all about moral values. They were certainly not about happy endings, although some were funny. Nevertheless I learnt a lot from them.

For example, in *The Girl Who Married a Ghost*, I learnt how pride comes before a fall. A beautiful girl was too proud to marry any of the men from her village, but eventually a ghost tricked her into marriage, and she suffered as a result. Then, in *The Wrestler and the Ghost*, I learnt about humility. A talented wrestler, not content with wrestling his fellow men, challenged a ghost in the land of the spirits to a wrestling march - and failed miserably.

The stories about Tortoise taught me other lessons. In *The Famine*, I learnt that lies always lead to trouble. Tortoise hid his food up a tree and never shared it with the other animals, then lied about it. But he paid the ultimate price when he was found out.... *Pig's Money* showed me that two wrongs can't make a right. Tortoise owed his friend Pig some money. When he failed to pay it back, Pig lost his temper and wrecked what he thought was Tortoise's furniture. As a result, he never got his money back. And *The Great Eating Competition* showed me that you can succeed if you're smart and observant, as I saw how Tortoise beat the other animals in eating the hot spicy food.

All the stories had important messages. *The Child Who Never Went Out* taught me about obedience, *Why the Lizard Nods his Head* showed me how greed will get you into trouble, *Who Stole Python's Eggs?* explained how wrong it is to steal, and in *Talented Grasshopper* I learnt about the futility of envy.

But most of all I learnt to love stories. The ones in this collection have stayed with me all my life, and I told them to my own children. Now I'm very happy to be able to share them with a new generation of readers, many of whom may never have been to Africa. Sometimes I've put the characters' words into Igbo, my own first language, because it feels more natural that way. But I've explained the meaning of the words in English too.

I hope you enjoy my stories.

The Great Eating Competition

A long time ago, life was rather dull in the jungle. The days were long and the animals didn't want to get out of bed in the morning. When they did, they had nothing new or exciting to do - until one day Lion, the king of the animals, had an idea to liven things up.

Mind you, he had to work hard to get the animals interested. First he asked Parrot to announce a meeting at his palace at six o'clock the next evening. Lion knew that meetings were best held at sunset, when a cool breeze blew gently through the jungle and everyone was more relaxed.

The next day at six o'clock the animals gathered at Lion's palace. Unfortunately the cool breeze hadn't relaxed them as Lion had hoped –

they arrived cross and grumpy, and whispered and squabbled among themselves.

Lion stood up. "*Ndibanyi kwenu!*" he shouted. "Greetings, everyone."

The animals muttered frostily, "*Ya!*"

"*Kwenu!*" shouted Lion again.

"*Ya!*" responded the animals, warming up a bit.

"Listen to me," said Lion. "Life is for living, not for moping around and feeling miserable. So, I tell you, ladies and gentlemen, you need to be happy. You need to do fun things!" He paused, to see if anyone was listening.

All the animals began to talk at once. Some were nodding their heads in agreement and others were disagreeing, shaking their heads vehemently.

Lion raised a paw and everyone fell silent. "Ladies and gentlemen, I'm introducing a new competition to the jungle. It is called The Great Eating Competition."

"This is a joke, right?" said Monkey, getting ready to leave.

Elephant laughed. "Look at me. I'll probably gobble up the whole lot before the competition even begins."

Giraffe was unimpressed too. "What's the point of watching each other stuff our mouths with food?" he scoffed. "Where's the excitement in that?"

Quite a few animals agreed with him, and soon they all began to squabble again.

"Listen, everyone," said Lion. "This competition will be different from all the others we've had before. I promise you it will be fun, and the rules are very simple. Please let me explain."

The animals listened. They were beginning to get interested.

Lion went on, "You're not allowed to drink water or talk while you're competing, and you must finish everything on your plate. And the winner will get a gold chain." He paused for a second. "What do you think? Are you with me so far?" he asked.

Some animals thought the rules were silly - they liked to drink water with their meals. But they liked the idea of the gold chain, and they agreed to give it a try.

On the day of the competition the animals hurried to the palace, and there stood a huge table draped in a white cloth.

The animals talked excitedly as they lined up and waited for the food to arrive. Elephant was the first in the queue - she couldn't wait to get that gold chain around her huge neck.

A few minutes later, Lion's wife brought in a huge plate piled high with food. The crowd cheered.

As the animals jostled for position in the queue, Lion went over the rules again. "Number one: you mustn't ask for water. Number two: you must not complain while eating the food. And number three: you must finish every scrap of food on the plate. Is that clear?"

The animals nodded their heads in unison.

Then Lion said, "I declare this competition now open!"

Elephant stepped forward and almost at once her mouth began to water. The food was her favourite: okra stew with plenty of vegetables.

Convinced that she was going to win, she scooped a large amount of stew into her mouth. But just then something strange happened. She began to hop on one leg and then the other. It was as if she was dancing on hot charcoal. She thought steam was coming out of her ears, and her mouth was on fire. Lion's wife must have put a thousand chillis into the food!

Elephant couldn't bear it any longer. "Water!" she screamed. "I want some water now!"

But by asking for water she had broken one of the rules and was out of the competition. She stepped aside for the next contestant.

Next came Giraffe. 'I'll do better than Elephant,' he told himself, 'it can't be that hard.'

The animals held their breath as Giraffe scooped a heap of food into his mouth. He took one bite and yelled for his mummy - his mouth and throat were on fire! He turned and fled.

One by one the animals went up to the table, but not one of them was able to finish the food. So they stood around in groups, wondering who could possibly win this tough competition.

"We mustn't give up," said Elephant, who'd now recovered from the effect of the chilli peppers.

At last there was just one animal left who hadn't tried to eat the food. It was Tortoise. But what could such a little animal do? He was far too small to win.

But Tortoise loved a good challenge. Also, he'd observed how the animals were tackling the competition, and he had an idea...

As he stepped forward, silence fell in the jungle. Everyone watched him closely, wondering how he'd deal with the chilli peppers.

Tortoise began with a question. "Please, Lion," he asked, "can I sing a song about this beautiful food, and about the chef who has cooked it?"

"By all means, Tortoise," said Lion. He didn't see anything wrong with singing. "Sing as much you like - as long as you finish what's on your plate."

So Tortoise taught all the animals how to sing the chorus to his song, and he told them to sing it as loud as they could.

He sang, "*Osili ofe n'osika!* Whoever cooked this sauce is a great chef!"

The animals responded, "*U. . . Ah!*"

Then Tortoise sang, *"Onye osili ñi n'osika!*
Whoever cooked this meal has outdone himself!"
and quickly stuffed some food into his mouth.

The animals responded again, *"U . . .Ah!"*
They liked his song.

Tortoise sang again, *"Osili ofe ñi n'osika!"* And
he stuffed some more food into his mouth just as
the animals were singing the chorus.

The louder the animals sang, the more Tortoise
was able to eat.

He carried on singing and eating, singing and
eating until his plate was empty. Immediately he
was declared the winner.

Clever Tortoise had outwitted Lion. Unknown
to anyone, he had been making lots of desperate
noises while he was eating the spicy food, which
meant he had broken one of the rules, but because
everyone was singing so loudly no one heard him
groaning or squealing!

All the animals jumped for joy. It had been a
long time since they'd had so much fun, and they
thanked Lion for organising the competition.

Lion hung a shiny new gold chain round
Tortoise's neck. And Elephant carried him on her
back so that everyone could see him.

And that was how Tortoise won the Great Eating Competition.

The moral of this story is - be very observant. Tortoise was able to size up the situation and learn from the mistakes of the other animals.

The Child Who
Never Went Out

There was once a man called Obinna and his wife Ngozi, who didn't have any children. They were miserable because they had no one to hug, to tell stories to, or even to share food with.

They sat in their silent house and stared into space. They had a big house, and without a child, it looked and felt abandoned. There was dust everywhere and cobwebs as thick as strings.

Eventually they went to see a doctor, and then more doctors. But none of them could find anything wrong. "Be patient," they said.

Then Obinna and Ngozi went back to their cold, miserable house, feeling upset and angry -

after all they'd been patient for a long time!

One day a neighbour suggested that Ngozi should visit a traditional healer. He was a short man with a head like a coconut, pointy at the top. He handed  her some herbs. "When you get home," he said, "boil these leaves and drink them."

Ngozi wasted no time at all. She snatched the herbs and ran all the way back to her house. Then she placed the herbs in a pot full of cold water and boiled them. Oh, how they stank! They smelt worse than five rotten eggs! But Ngozi was brave - she drank the whole lot in one gulp.

Several months went by, and nothing happened. Ngozi went to see another healer, and then another, until she'd seen twenty. Some gave her bitter herbs to drink, while others gave her herbs to bathe in. No matter how they tasted or smelled, Ngozi took them all. And still she had no children.

But she never gave up wishing that one day her dreams would come true. And one day they did - but in a most surprising way...

One night, feeling sad, Ngozi sat in front of her house and began to sob. All the neighbours heard her, but they were too scared to come out and comfort her because it was pitch black outside. Even the moon and stars stayed away that night. Worse still, it was past midnight, when spirits and ghosts roam about.

Maybe someone should have told Ngozi to keep quiet, because a few minutes later, strange things began to happen. First the wind began to blow. It shook the leaves on the trees and scattered those on the ground. One leaf blew into Ngozi's face, making her gasp for air. She stopped crying at once. Then everything went quiet and the wind dropped.

And now Ngozi heard footsteps approaching.

She peered into the darkness. "Who's there?" she said shakily.

Whoever it was remained silent.

"Who's there?" Ngozi asked again, terrified.

At last, a voice as sweet as honey replied, "I am the spirit of your ancestors."

"Oh, Mama," said Ngozi in relief, thinking it was the voice of her dead mother. "Thank you for coming. You heard me crying and you've come to help me."

Smiling now, Ngozi took a few steps forward, but the voice said sharply, "Stop, you mustn't come any further!"

Ngozi stood still.

"I heard you crying," the voice said gently, "and I came to help you. You'll soon have a child, trust me."

Now Ngozi began to dance with joy. "I'm going to have a child, I'm going to be a mother!" she sang to herself.

The voice interrupted her. "Tomorrow morning I want you to go to the market and buy the finest palm oil you can find. Wait until midnight, and then pour the oil on the ground in front of your house. When you wake up in the morning you'll find a child standing on your veranda. But you must never, never let this child out in the sun. Remember, oil melts in the heat."

And the unknown spirit faded away.

The next morning Ngozi leapt out of bed and rushed to the market to buy palm oil. She bought the very best oil she could find.

She waited till midnight, as she'd been told, then she poured the palm oil on the ground, right in front of her house.

At daybreak Ngozi ran outside. There, standing on the veranda, was a beautiful child with her arms outstretched, wanting to be picked up.

The oil had turned into a little girl.

"What a beautiful, beautiful child you are!" said Ngozi, sweeping the child into her arms. How could anything made of oil be so perfect?

She held the child for what seemed like forever before letting go. Then curiosity got the better of her. She took the girl's hand and examined it closely. She wanted to know if anyone would be able to tell that her child was made of oil. She even sniffed her arm, but amazingly the child looked and smelt like any normal four-year-old. No one would have guessed she was made out of palm oil.

"You're truly beautiful!" Ngozi said again, and she took the child inside to show her to her husband, who was astonished and delighted.

The little girl had such lovely skin! It was as smooth as a pebble and as rich as palm oil - a deep orangey-red colour. Obinna and Ngozi named her Apunanwụ (Never go out in the sun), to remind themselves that this little girl could never go outside, especially when it was sunny.

Apunanwụ's parents loved her dearly. They gave her lots of toys to play with. She had enough to fill a shop! She even had her own playground. And why not, since she had to spend her life indoors? Her father built the playground in the middle of their sitting room. He knocked down a few walls, took out the chairs and tables, and replaced them with a slide, a swing, a climbing frame and a sand pit. Apunanwụ played there often.

She even had her own indoor garden. As she didn't go to school like the other children, she had plenty of time to explore all the different plants in her garden. She could pick as many flowers as she liked.

If she ever grew bored playing in the playground or in the garden, she'd go to her maze. Her father had built her a marvellous maze in one of the spare rooms, with lots of tunnels, all made out of mud bricks. Apunanwụ spent ages trying to work out how to find her way through it. And she also spent time doing pottery, carving, drawing and painting.

Apunanwụ was happy for a while, but more and more she longed to go outside. One day she went to her mother and said, "Mama, please may I go outside and play? Please, Mama!"

Her mother came and sat next to her. Then she said very gently, "My child, I cannot let you go outside."

"Why, Mama?"

"Because you're a special child," Ngozi said,

hoping that would be the end of the matter.

But Apunanwụ persisted. "Why am I a special child, Mama?"

Her mother's stomach tied itself into a knot. She was scared to tell her daughter the truth. At last she said again, "You must never go outside, do you hear me? Never!"

Tears rolled down Apunanwụ's face, and she clung to her mother. She asked again, "Why can't I go outside? All the other children go outside except me. Why?"

Her mother took a deep breath. "My child," she said, "you're special because you're made from palm oil. And if you ever go outside, you will melt and we won't have you any more."

Apunanwụ took a step back; she knew what palm oil was, she'd seen her mother cook with it many times, and she'd eaten it in her food. In fact, her favourite meal was yam dipped in palm oil with a little salt and pepper.

She stared at her hands and legs to see if they were different from her mother's. And indeed they were! While her mother's skin tone was dark, hers was the colour of palm oil: a beautiful deep red mixed with dark orange.

Apunanwụ sobbed like a lost child. And her mother comforted her, hugging her tightly and whispering over and over again that she loved her. Finally, she promised she would never leave Apunanwụ on her own.

***

For several years Ngozi kept her promise and stayed with Apunanwụ every day. However the time came, when the girl was older, that her mother had to go back to work to help her husband on their farm.

The first time both parents went out to work, it was for just a couple of hours, and Apunanwụ was quite happy. The second time, they spent three hours at the farm, and still Apunanwụ didn't mind.

But the third time, Obinna and Ngozi spent a long time at the farm, and the poor girl started to feel very lonely. After five hours she went to sit by the window so that she would see her parents returning.

She'd only been there for a couple of minutes when she noticed two children playing quite close to her house. Apunanwụ watched as the children did skipping, cartwheels and jumping. She could tell they were having fun because they were laughing. How she wished she could play with them!

At that very moment one of the children saw her and came over to talk to her.

Apunanwụ opened the window.

"You can come and play with us if you like," the girl said.

But Apunanwụ remembered that her mother had warned her never to go outside. She thanked the girl, but said she would not come out. Then she closed the window and went to play by herself.

Another hour passed and still her parents hadn't come back. Apunanwụ went back to the window. The children were still playing, and again she watched them longingly.

Soon, the same child asked once more if she'd like to join them.

Apunanwụ hesitated, but this time she said yes. Surely it would be all right, she thought, if she played with the children for just a few minutes.

She opened the door and stepped outside for the first time in her life! A sweet breeze blew gently on her face, and it felt wonderful. The sun had disappeared behind a cloud.

Apunanwụ played happily with the children. She began to enjoy herself so much, she didn't notice that the sun had come out from behind the clouds, and was now blazing down.

After a few more minutes her new friends said they were going home. It was getting too hot to play. But Apunanwụ was enjoying herself too much to stop. She carried on playing by herself, out in the sunshine.

It grew hotter and hotter, and finally she decided to go back indoors. But when she tried to walk, she couldn't move. Her legs were like chewing-gum, stuck firmly to the ground. The more she tried to lift one leg off the ground, the more it stuck. She bent down to see what the trouble was, and discovered the leg had stretched so much it was now longer than the other one.

So she tried lifting the other leg off the ground, but it too stretched like chewing-gum.

She was melting!

Apunanwụ looked down at her hands and saw that they had changed shape. They were getting longer and longer, until all her fingers merged into two thin stumps. Puzzled, she stared at them, and then she remembered her mother's warning.

Poor Apunanwụ! Her face began to drip with oil, and gradually her whole body melted. Soon all that was left was a pool of palm oil.

When her parents came home they called her name and searched everywhere for her. But Apunanwụ was nowhere to be found. At last they saw the pool of palm oil in front of their house and at once they realized what had happened.

Ngozi began to cry and cry. She sat down by the pool of oil, and then she sang this lament for her daughter . . .

O. . o. . o . . co
Co. . co. . o . . o
Ude mmili mu ezuwe! (My oil has melted!)
Akwali wali! (What a loss!)
Ude mmili mu ezuwe!

Ngozi sang for a long time, calling for her lost child.

But Apunanwụ had gone back to the spirit world, and there was nothing anyone could do about it.

The moral of this story is - always listen to your parents and do as they tell you.

Lazy Dog
and Tortoise

Many years ago, there was a water shortage in the jungle, and it caused a lot of misery for the animals. Elephant couldn't have any more mud baths, and all the animals were thirsty. And none of them knew how long the water crisis was going to last. They were all very worried.

The animals also had to deal with the burning heat. Even the lovely breeze, that used to rustle the leaves on the trees while cooling the animals, had stopped. The animals knew they had to do something to avoid a disaster in the jungle.

First they decided to look for water in other areas. They explored caves, valleys, hills and plains. But all they found were piles of stones, rocks and dead plants.

Next the animals decided to try water rationing, which meant that every animal would get a certain amount of water according to the size of their family. Naturally, larger families got more water, and this soon created a lot of problems. And there was another difficulty: the most popular animals got more water than the unpopular ones. In the end many had almost nothing.

Quarrels broke out amongst the animals, and some started stealing water from others. Fighting broke out everywhere – it was terrible.

If only it would rain! Tirelessly the animals searched the sky for signs of rain. Sometimes they saw clouds gathering and got very excited – but it never rained. It was as if the weather was teasing them.

One morning, as disaster was looming like a dark cloud over their heads, Tortoise had an idea. He'd woken up with his mind as sharp as a brand new knife, and he knew exactly what he had to do. He, Tortoise, was going to dig a well which would bring the water shortage to an end!

But he'd need help if his idea was to become a reality, and so he set off to see his new friend, Dog. He and Dog had become good friends about a month ago, but Tortoise felt he knew him well enough to ask for help.

When Tortoise arrived, his friend was still in bed, but he got up and offered him a chair.

Tortoise came straight to the point. "Listen, I have a great plan that will solve the water shortage," he said.

"What is your plan?" asked Dog eagerly.

"A well," answered the tortoise.

Dog shook his head. He didn't like the sound of that - he was already thinking of all the work it would involve. His ears flopped down like an empty plastic bag.

You see, Dog was very lazy. He loved nothing better than to curl up in a ball and sleep all day. But he was desperate for water, and he listened patiently as Tortoise explained his new plan.

"I know a good place for a well. I think there's plenty of water just below the surface. So, here is what we have to do. First we need tools for digging a hole. We'll get those from Lion - he has lots of tools."

Dog was getting increasingly worried.

"Don't worry," soothed Tortoise. "Think of all the drinking water we'll have - litres and litres of it, my dear friend!"

Dog began to dream of drinking a cool glass of water for the first time in days. "Ok, when shall we start?" he said, jumping up happily. He danced and sang, "*Ezigbo mmili*! Lovely natural water. We're going to have *ezigbo mmili*! Oh, sweet drinking water, pure drinking water!"

Tortoise was happy too. "Let's start first thing tomorrow morning," he said. "Don't forget - we need an axe, two shovels and perhaps a bucket."

Dog nodded his head, but he wasn't listening. He was too busy thinking about quenching his parched throat.

Tortoise turned to him. "Shall we meet first thing in the morning then? We'll go together to get the tools. I'll see you at the old guava tree near Lion's house."

"No, problem, I'll be there," said Dog.

Tortoise left his friend's house humming a song. He was feeling very happy indeed. He knew his plan was going to work with the help of his friend. He hadn't told the other animals yet, and he imagined the look of surprise on their faces when they saw the well.

***

Next morning, Tortoise set off bright and early for the old guava tree. The sun was just rising from behind a few trees on the horizon when he got there. But Dog was nowhere to be seen. So Tortoise settled down to wait for him. He waited and waited.

The minutes turned into hours and the temperature rose sharply. Tortoise feared that if he continued to sit there the well would never be dug, so he went to get the tools by himself.

When he came back, Dog was still not there, and Tortoise decided to pay him a visit.

Loaded down with tools he arrived at Dog's house, and found him sleeping. He showed him the tools.

Dog yawned sleepily. "You'd better get started," he said. "I'll join you as soon as I can."

So Tortoise left, carrying the tools. He found an ideal place for a well and began digging the ground. He dug and dug, and the hole got deeper and deeper. By and by some of the animals came out and helped him. Some even brought their own buckets. They formed a long chain, passing bucketsful of sand down the line for emptying.

At last there was a trickle of water, then more, and the well was finished. Now the animals had enough water to drink, and for washing too.

Next day Dog appeared with his bucket. He drew some water from the well, and began to drink it. But when Tortoise saw him he ran straightaway to tell Lion. He didn't see why Dog should drink water from the well when he'd done absolutely nothing to help.

Lion accompanied Tortoise to the well, and there they found Dog still drinking.

"What are you doing here?" asked Lion.

"Drinking water of course!" said Dog nonchalently.

"You didn't help with the digging of this well, did you?" said Lion. "You let your friend down after promising you'd help him."

Dog ignored him and carried on drinking.

Lion spoke again. "I want you to say you're sorry for your behaviour - or else!"

"Or else what?" said Dog defiantly, his eyes blazing with anger.

"Say sorry, or I'll stop you drinking from this well."

But Dog took no notice at all. He wasn't afraid of one little threat.

Then Lion let out a great roar, and strode towards him. Now Dog was really scared. He fled like a coward; he ran as fast as his four legs could carry him. He was terrified of Lion.

Lion waited for Dog to come back and say sorry, but he never did. And none of the animals ever saw Dog again.

The moral of this story is - laziness won't get you anywhere!

The Girl Who Married a Ghost

Many years ago, there was a pretty little girl who always did exactly what she wished. If she wanted to stay indoors all day, she stayed in, no matter how much her friends begged her to come out to play. And if she didn't want to speak to anyone for a whole week, she didn't say a word until seven days had passed!

The girl's name was Ogilisa and she lived in a small village where everyone knew everyone else.

When Ogilisa was five years old, she chose all the best-looking children in the village to be her friends. When they came to her house, Ogilisa chose the games they played. And her friends didn't mind playing Ogilisa's games, because they admired her so much. In their eyes she could do no wrong.

As Ogilisa grew older, she looked more and more beautiful. Her eyes were like almonds, her skin as smooth as a pebble fresh out of the sea. She rarely smiled, but when she did, it was as if an angel was smiling at you.

Ogilisa had lovely hair too – long, shiny and soft. When she said she wanted beads to put in her hair, her friends fell over each other in the rush to give her the prettiest beads they possessed.

By the time Ogilisa was eighteen, people began calling her a goddess, and they took their newborn babies to be blessed by her. By now she thought she was more important than anyone else, and she grew pompous, self-centred and proud. And like all goddesses, she thought she could do what she liked....

***

One hot day when the sun was blazing down, Ogilisa decided she was going to get married. She went to tell her parents, who were sitting in the shade of a mango tree.

"Arrange a wedding for me – at once!" she cried.

Her parents said no, she was too young. On hearing this, Ogilisa had a big tantrum and smashed everything in the house. Clay pots, bottles, mirrors, she broke them all. Then she threw herself on the ground and wailed.

Her parents couldn't bear it any longer, and they gave in to their daughter. They called the town crier, who summoned all the young men to the village square and announced that Ogilisa was looking for a husband.

When the young men heard the news, they ran off to iron their best clothes. In less than an hour they were on their way to Ogilisa's house.

The first man puffed out his chest like a peacock, and swaggered towards Ogilisa, convinced she would choose him.

But Ogilisa took one look at him and cried, "Look at you, your ears are too big! I don't want to marry someone who reminds me of an elephant!"

The poor man slunk away, ashamed.

The second suitor, whose neck was covered in gold chains, strode boldly up to Ogilisa.

But his gold had no effect on Ogilisa.

She shook her lovely head, and said, "Look at your skinny little legs. I don't want to marry someone who reminds me of a crane."

And to the third man she said, "Look at your eyes, they're too big. I won't marry someone who looks like an owl!"

One by one all the men filed past Ogilisa, but not a single one would suit her. Either they had mouths like goldfish or heads like bicycle seats. Something was wrong with each of them.

Finally, Ogilisa had had enough. "Stupid village!" she yelled. "I should have known that there's no man on this earth good enough for me!"

But Ogilisa should never have said those words, because it was night-time, when ghosts start to roam the countryside.

At that very moment a ghost was wafting through the village. He heard Ogilisa. "Ha!" he thought. "I'm going to teach this silly girl a lesson. I'll marry her!"

But the ghost had a problem – he was invisible.

There was only one thing to do: the ghost had to find some body parts and pretend he was human. And with that in mind, he went out looking for someone – anyone foolish enough to be out and about late at night.

It wasn't long before the ghost came across a drunken man lying helpless in a gutter, cursing his useless legs. "I might as well not have any legs at all," he muttered to himself.

The ghost heard him, and was only too happy to rid the man of his legs. He tore them off the man's body like pieces of paper, and the man was too drunk to feel a thing!

Now the ghost went in search of other body parts.

Soon he came across a man wandering the street, cursing his arms and crying, "I hate these arms. I wish I had arms like other men instead of these weak sticks."

At once the ghost tore off the man's arms, and for some strange reason the man didn't feel a thing; and nor did the man whose hair was pulled from his scalp.

Then the ghost went in search of a head and a body. After all, a ghost needs to attach hair and limbs to something!

Soon he found a body, a head, a nose, eyeballs, lips, ears – everything he needed to look human, including clothes. Then he came across an empty car, and drove to Ogilisa's house.

At midnight he knocked on her door.

When Ogilisa opened the door she thought she must be dreaming. There, standing before her, was the most handsome man she had ever seen. She didn't waste time asking where the man had come from. Instead she yelled, "Mama, Papa, come and see the man I'm going to marry!"

Ogilisa's parents welcomed the man inside and

offered him food. But Ogilisa wanted to get married at once. So they called out the local priest, and he carried out a quick ceremony for them before going back to bed.

After the wedding, Ogilisa's new husband said, "We must go, we have a long journey ahead of us."

He got up to leave, and Ogilisa followed. She was at the door in the blink of an eye!

"Why not wait until morning?" said Ogilisa's parents. "It's not safe driving at night."

But Ogilisa's husband ignored their pleas and took Ogilisa out to the car. He drove through the village like a maniac. Ogilisa had to clutch the seat to stop herself flying through the roof. He carried on speeding until they came to a junction, where he stopped suddenly. He said he needed to see someone, and got out of the car.

Ogilisa sat alone, waiting for him. The moon was shining brightly and there were bats everywhere. Some flew within a few feet of her and owls stared down at her.

Suddenly a tiny bird perched on the car window and began to sing. Ogilisa clapped her hands loudly and the bird flew away. Perhaps she should have listened to what the bird was saying, but Ogilisa never paid attention to what anyone said, let alone a bird.

A few seconds later, her husband appeared. But he looked different. Instead of walking, he was shuffling along on his bottom.

"What happened to you?" complained Ogilisa. "And where have you been all this time?"

As he came closer, she saw that he had no legs! She screamed loudly, and her husband explained that some horrible people had chopped off his legs.

Ogilisa felt sorry for him, and as he could no longer drive the car, she drove instead.

After they'd gone a few miles, he asked Ogilisa to stop the car, because he had to see someone else. He shuffled off behind some thick bushes.

As soon as he was out of sight, the tiny bird

perched on the car window again.

This time the bird sang its song more slowly so that Ogilisa could understand what it was saying.

It sang,

Ogilisa akwọlu aka, tụmalụ tụmalụ n'gwe,
Esokwana, esokwana je!
(Ogilisa, don't follow this man!)

But Ogilisa clapped her hands so noisily the bird got scared and flew away.

This time, when her husband came back, he had no nose and was a bald as an egg. Ogilisa didn't like ugly men, and this man was surely the ugliest man alive.

"What's wrong with you?" she shouted. "From the moment we married, you've been falling apart!"

Her husband didn't want to tell her he was returning all those body parts he'd borrowed. So he told her another lie.

They drove on, and ten minutes later the man shuffled off again.

Now the bird appeared to Ogilisa for a third time. It sang the same song to her again,

Ogilisa akwǫlu aka, tụmalụ tụmalụ n'gwe,
Esokwana, esokwana je!

This time Ogilisa listened and understood. All at once she realised what had happened.

"I've married a ghost!" she cried, and she was so frightened she ran all the way home. Had she turned around she would have seen that the man she'd married had turned into a slimy, sticky grey paste.

She told her parents everything; she hung her head in shame and apologised for not listening to them.

And from that day onwards, Ogilisa stopped being selfish and arrogant. She wasn't perfect, but she became a much nicer person.

Marrying a ghost had certainly taught her a lesson!

The moral of this story is - don't be too choosy because you never know what you might get!

Pig's Money

Many, many years ago Pig and Tortoise were best friends. They went everywhere together, and did everything together. In fact, they were like two seeds in an udala fruit. You'd never see one without the other. They spent hours and hours in each other's company - a day never went by without the two meeting up for a chat.

Over the years the other animals began to refer to them as brothers. "Where is your brother?" they'd ask Pig, if they saw him without his friend.

But sadly, like most things in this world, Pig and Tortoise's friendship didn't last for ever...

***

It all began one afternoon when Tortoise went to visit Pig.

"Please, my friend," said Tortoise, in a voice coated with sweet honey, "will you lend me some money? I'll pay you back next Tuesday."

Pig's heart melted with sympathy. He was truly sorry to hear that his friend was short of money. "Of course I'll lend you some," he said to Tortoise. "You're my best friend!"

Tortoise smiled. He was relieved and grateful. He had been very worried that Pig might not have enough money to lend him.

"Now, tell me how much you need," said Pig.

"Please could you lend me 2000 Naira?" asked Tortoise. "I'll pay you back next Tuesday, and that's a promise!"

Pig went into his bedroom and lifted up his

pillow, where he kept all his money. He counted out the exact amount and put the pillow back in place. Then he took the cash to Tortoise. "Here you are, my friend," he said kindly.

Tortoise thanked him profusely, and promised again to pay it all back the following Tuesday.

But when Tuesday came, Tortoise failed to pay back the money to his friend. Instead he made an excuse.

"My poor mother is very sick in hospital," he said in a mournful voice.

Pig felt sorry for him. "That's all right, my friend," he said, "just pay me next week."

But Tortoise didn't pay back the money the following week. This time his excuse was that his father was very ill. And as the months went by, he gave Pig all kinds of excuses for not paying back the money he owed.

At last Pig's sympathy ran out – he was tired of his friend's excuses.

"Why do you keep lying to me?" he snapped. "I've been generous and kind to you – but now I want my money back!"

Once again Tortoise promised to pay him the following week, but this time, when he failed to do so, Pig took action. Early one morning, as the sun was rising, he set off to his friend's house, determined to get his money back no matter what.

Tortoise was at home, relaxing. He'd just had his breakfast, and was sitting in his garden, under a mango tree. Now this tree was quite close to the road, surrounded by thick shrubs. Tortoise was well hidden there, but he could see any animals that came along before they could see him!

As he sat on his reclining chair he heard a grunting sound close by. Tortoise sat up and looked around. Suddenly he felt a cold chill at the back of his neck: there, at the end of his footpath and moving at an alarming speed, was Pig!

"Oh no!" panicked Tortoise. "What shall I do?"

He retreated to his house, thinking fast. And within seconds, he had come up with a brilliant plan.

His wife was busy chopping vegetables for lunch. Suddenly she heard Tortoise shouting from the doorway, "Wife, turn me over. Turn me over now!"

Baffled by the panic in her husband's voice, she just stared at him.

Tortoise began to shake like a leaf. "For goodness' sake, wife, turn me over on my back, quickly!"

His wife was still puzzled by his strange behaviour, but she snapped into action. She heaved the small creature on to his back. Now Tortoise was lying on his shell with his legs in the air like an overturned beetle. But he didn't mind looking silly, as long as Pig didn't spot him.

Then he said, "Wife, get your chopping board and put it on my belly and start chopping the vegetables."

His wife did as he told her. She took the chopping board, placed it on Tortoise's tummy and began chopping the vegetables.

Just at that moment Pig came in.

"Where is your husband?" he grunted fiercely, glaring at the strange table.

"He's not in," said Tortoise's wife calmly.

"Where's he gone?" asked the pig furiously.

"I don't know," said Tortoise's wife, without looking up.

At once, all the anger that Pig had held back during those weeks waiting for his money, rose up in him. With one swift movement he picked up the strange table, lifted it high in the air and threw it like a ball out of the window. The table flew in the air for a second and landed outside.

Tortoise tried not to cry out from the burning pain in his back. He'd landed with a thud on the hard ground.

But Pig hadn't finished yet. He turned to Tortoise's wife, and in a voice that would send any animal running for cover, he warned, "I'm coming back tomorrow to get my money, you hear me?"

Then he left.

Tortoise lay still for a few more minutes to make sure Pig had gone, before picking himself up. Then he went back inside. Fortunately, he wasn't too badly hurt.

His wife was scared. She told him Pig would be back the next day.

"Good!" said Tortoise, already thinking of his next plan.

The next morning, the angry pig came back, and this time he found Tortoise at home, relaxing.

Tortoise smiled as he saw Pig approaching. He didn't run away at all. He just waited quietly as his friend came closer and closer.

Pig felt very uneasy. Tortoise was up to something - he looked too relaxed. Nevertheless, he yelled, "Where is my money, you thief? I need my money now!"

But Tortoise very calmly said, "And where is my table? I need my table now. My wife told me you threw my precious table out of the window."

"OK, I'll get you your stupid little table," said Pig contemptuously. "But I still want my money back!"

He stormed off outside to look for the table. He went round the house to where he thought it might have landed, but it wasn't there. He went to the other side of the house, in case it might have been moved. Still he couldn't find it. For about thirty minutes he searched for the table, all to no avail.

Finally he came back into the house. "I'm very sorry, I don't know what happened to your table," he muttered sheepishly.

"Oh, what a pity!" said Tortoise. "I could have given you back your money right now if only you'd found my table…"

Poor Pig had to leave without his money – and Tortoise never did pay back the money he owed him.

The moral of this story is - stay calm, otherwise you'll be like the angry Pig who never got back his money.

The Famine

A long time ago, all the animals were very worried and scared. In fact, they were so scared they couldn't sleep at night. You see, there was a big food shortage in the forest, and this meant a lot of the animals were going to bed hungry.

Before this wretched situation began, food was plentiful and the animals could eat whatever they wanted. In those days life was sweet and everyone was blissfully happy. There was sunshine, blue sky, a beautiful river, and a jungle filled with all kinds of trees and plants.

Then one day everything changed. The leaves on the trees turned yellow and dropped to the ground, the plants withered and died, and the entire forest was as hot as an oven! With the temperature rising sky high, the river began to dry up and the animals struggled to find water.

Food began to grow scarce, and the animals became fearful and anxious. Some of them lost a lot of weight. But it wasn't just the weight loss - they lost their tempers too and got into fights. Those that weren't fighting stole food from other animals. It was a horrendous situation.

Lion, the king of the jungle, had no choice but to call a meeting. Perhaps he could persuade the animals to stop hoarding food, and share what they had. Then things would be better…

The animals all hoped that Lion would offer them a magic solution to the food crisis, and they came to the meeting with high hopes. But they were soon disappointed.

"*Ndibanyi kwenu!*" roared Lion. "Greetings, everyone!"

The hungry animals answered, "*Ya!*"

"*Kwenu!*" Lion roared a second time.

"*Ya!*" shouted the animals.

When he had their full attention, Lion said, "I called you here today because of our food crisis. We must do something about it!"

The animals nodded their heads in agreement.

"I suggest you bring all your food to me," went on Lion.

"What?" said one animal in disbelief.

Another animal rushed forward. "Now he wants to steal all our food," he said loudly. "Well, I'm not having that."

"This meeting is a complete waste of time," said Monkey furiously. "I'm going home to hide my food."

"Quiet!" roared Lion. "Let me explain. Let's all bring our food together, and share it. I'll start by bringing my food and sharing it with you."

This seemed to calm the animals – all except Tortoise. You see, he was convinced that Lion wanted to trick the other animals out of their precious food. So while most of the animals celebrated Lion's idea with a dance, Tortoise was busy thinking of a secret place where he could hide his food.

Aha! An idea came to him like a flash of lightning. He would pretend he had no food at all.

So Tortoise said in a shaky voice, "I have no food. I have nothing to share with you all. I'm very sorry."

It was enough to soften the hardest heart. At once, all the animals surrounded him, saying, "Oh you poor thing! Don't worry, we'll take care of you."

Tortoise couldn't resist one last tug at their heartstrings. "Shake me up and down if you think I am lying," he said. "Go on, shake me like an *ishaka*, and hear me rattle in my shell, because I'm so thin and hungry!"

Lion hugged Tortoise, crying, "Oh you poor creature! No one is going to shake you up and down, I promise. Listen, don't worry about food. You can have some of ours any time you want."

Tortoise smiled to himself. All he had to do now was sit back and enjoy their food without sharing his. He wished he could dance to celebrate, but of course then he would be found out.

When the meeting was over, the animals rushed home to bring their food for sharing. They put it in sacks and set off to Lion's house.

They reached his den as the sun was disappearing over the horizon. Lion quickly divided the food into tiny pieces, but saved some for another day. Then he handed each animal a small portion of food.

For the first time in months everyone had something to eat.

After dinner Tortoise said he was going home to sleep, but instead he hid behind a huge tree and sang a song. Whoever heard of an animal singing at a time of famine? Anyway, Tortoise sang,

Nne tụ da ụdọ (Mother, throw down the rope),
Tụ da ụdọ (Throw down the rope),
Tụ da ụdọ,
Ọnye welu nkeya o debe
(Every animal for himself),
Tụ da ụdọ.

He sang and sang until a rope as thick as a hose fell from the top of the tree to the ground. Tortoise grabbed it and began to climb. He climbed and climbed, right up to the top of the tree. This was where his mother lived, in a house on a strong tree branch, well hidden from view.

A delicious smell drifted towards Tortoise as he went inside. He hurried to the table, and sat down. Within seconds, his mother brought him a huge dish of delicious moi-moi meal. Tortoise gobbled up everything on his plate. His mother piled more food on his plate, and he gobbled that up too. Soon, he'd eaten enough to feed ten guests!

But that wasn't the end of his dinner. He ate some sweet mangoes and oranges for pudding, and even licked his plate! Smacking his lips noisily,

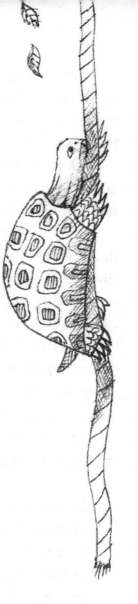

Tortoise left the table and, with his belly the size of a small bag of yams, he staggered to the rope and made his way slowly down.

The next day Tortoise sang the same song and went up the tree again. Every time he was hungry, he'd sing the song and the rope would be thrown down. Then he'd eat and eat until his stomach was close to bursting.

Soon he looked like Humpty Dumpty. His belly was fat and his cheeks were the size of two small balloons. Moving around the jungle became quite a job for fat Tortoise. But it didn't stop him eating!

One afternoon, as he waddled this way and that, he bumped into Elephant. He'd been whistling a tune, unaware that the thin elephant was round the corner, searching for food.

Elephant said to him, "Why are you so happy at a time of famine?"

"Why, my friend," replied the fat tortoise, "I'm always happy!"

Elephant was suspicious. 'Look at him,' she thought, 'he's put on a lot of weight. He must be getting extra food from somewhere.'

Eventually she said to him, "How come you're so fat, Tortoise?"

For a moment it looked as if Tortoise's plan would be discovered. Quickly he said with a broad smile, "It's the air, my friend!"

Elephant was furious. "What do you mean, the air? I breathe the same air as you, but I'm not fat!"

"I'm telling you it's the air!" insisted Tortoise. Then he waddled off, praying that Elephant wouldn't ask him any more tricky questions.

The next day he bumped into thin Snake. Like Elephant, she was out searching for food. Tortoise, as usual, had just finished a huge meal, and was whistling a cheerful tune.

Again he was asked why he was so fat, and again he replied, "It's the air, my friend."

But Snake was not convinced, and she vowed to keep an eye on him. Was Tortoise's plan about to unravel?

A few hours later Snake saw Tortoise climbing the tree, and she hurried off to tell Lion. But unfortunately Lion didn't believe her. Snake was known throughout the jungle for telling tall tales.

Days went by and Tortoise continued to eat well. By now he was eating every hour. He'd go up the tree for lunch, and a few minutes later he'd be back for some snacks. It was ridiculous when the other animals were starving!

As time went on, Tortoise began to take risks, and he sang his song ever more loudly. Perhaps he didn't care any more if he was caught.

Finally, all the animals began to notice something odd about Tortoise. He was the only animal who never seemed to complain of hunger. Could he be hiding food somewhere?

Monkey decided to spy on him, so the next day he followed Tortoise, keeping well out of sight. Soon, he saw him climbing a rope hanging from a tree, and he ran quickly to tell Lion.

Sadly, Lion didn't believe him either. Monkey had a reputation for exaggerating things. He'd often describe something as being huge when it was really just a tiny thing.

But a few days later Tortoise's secret was discovered, and this is how it happened....

One cloudy morning, Lion himself witnessed Tortoise singing and waddling along, and he decided to send Giraffe to find out what Tortoise was up to.

Giraffe was well suited for the job. She was calm and sensible, and besides, her height meant that she could see things the other animals couldn't.

She followed Tortoise, and very soon she spotted him climbing the rope up to the tree house. Giraffe waited calmly until Tortoise reached the top. Then she stretched her long neck to see what he was doing.

There was Tortoise, settled in a comfortable chair and eating from a huge bowl. What's more, there was lots of different food on the table.

Giraffe had seen enough. She galloped straight to Lion's house.

This time Lion believed the story. He gathered all the animals together, and they marched to the spot where Giraffe had seen Tortoise. Then they waited silently for the culprit to climb down.

Sure enough, a few minutes later, Tortoise began his slow descent, clutching the thick rope as he lowered himself down. He had no idea he wasn't alone.

When he was halfway down the rope, Lion roared so loudly that the whole jungle shook.

"Come down here at once!" he roared like thunder.

Fat Tortoise almost jumped out of his shell. He looked down, and got such a fright that he lost his grip - and began to fall. Many pairs of eyes watched as the Humpty-Dumpty Tortoise tumbled down the tree.

He tried to save himself by clawing the air, but it was hopeless; he was travelling at the speed of lightning. The wind whipped his fat cheeks, and he wailed, "Help, help me!"

Then he hit the hard ground with a loud THUD!

Poor Tortoise! He'd landed on his back, and his shell was broken into pieces. He was in great pain.

Lion picked him up and said, "If you don't tell me what you were doing up that tree, I won't mend your shell."

Well, at first Tortoise tried to say that he'd climbed the tree to get a better view of the jungle. Then he said he was looking for something to eat. But at last he admitted that he stored food at the top of the tree. He said he was very sorry for lying to the animals, and for not sharing his food.

In the end, Lion mended his broken shell using some gum from a tree, and grateful Tortoise took all the animals up the tree for a feast. And after that he always shared his food!

The moral of this story is – you mustn't be greedy. You must share what you have with others, especially those who have none.

Who Stole
Python's Eggs?

A long time ago, Python was the most miserable
animal in the jungle. She was under stress and
deeply suspicious of everyone and everything.

You see, each time she laid her eggs they'd
disappear like a puff of smoke. Someone or
something was stealing them but she had no idea
who was responsible.

It all began one fine day, when Python laid
some eggs in the middle of a cornfield. At the time
it seemed like a safe place. Row upon row of corn
with their long leaves and stems, hid her. And for
a while it *was* safe - until she went off to look for
something to eat. She was starving. When she came

back a few minutes later, she discovered her eggs had disappeared.

Shocked and angry, Python began to look for the thief who had stolen her precious eggs.

After a few minutes she heard a crunching sound, as if someone was eating a lettuce. Python followed the sound. She was convinced someone was eating her eggs and their shells.

However, standing quite still with only his jaw moving from side to side, was Goat. He was unaware Python was watching him.

"Why are you eating my eggs?" said Python.

Goat's jaw dropped wide open, revealing bits of half chewed food. He was horrified. How could his friend accuse him of such a thing?

"Look!" he said sternly. "I didn't eat any eggs. If you must know, I'm eating an ear of a corn."

Embarrassed, Python turned around quickly, muttering, "Next time I'm going to find a much safer place for my eggs."

A few weeks later, Python found a perfect place. It was behind a tall palm tree. She laid her eggs, and again went to look for something to eat. She was starving!

When she came back, her eggs had disappeared.

"Who is doing this to me?" cried Python.

Indeed, who stole Python's eggs?

She began searching for the thief. After a few seconds she heard something - it was a rustling sound, as if someone was walking across a pile of dried leaves. Python rushed to investigate!

A few yards from the palm tree she saw Squirrel. Her claws were clasped together and she was munching something. Something that was very delicious. Seeing bits of food dropping down from the sides of Squirrel's tiny mouth, Python became convinced she was eating her eggs.

"Squirrel!" yelled Python. "Are you eating my eggs?"

Squirrel put down her food. "What do you mean?" she said angrily. "I'm not eating your eggs. I'm eating some nuts!"

So, who stole Python's eggs?

Feeling very embarrassed and guilty, Python beat a hasty retreat. She didn't like accusing her friends of stealing, but she was getting desperate.

'Next time I must find somewhere even safer,' she said to herself.

A month later, Python found another place, and it was perfect. It was surrounded by banana trees. Everyone who knows banana trees will tell you they grow in clusters, so it was a very good place for Python's eggs.

She laid her eggs.

But after some minutes she became very hungry. She looked around to make sure no one had seen her, before leaving to find something to eat. But when she came back, the eggs had gone. Poor Python cried and cried.

So, who stole those eggs?

Python suddenly heard some leaves rustling a few feet above her and stopped crying. She looked up and saw Monkey swinging from one tree branch to another like an acrobat in a circus.

"Monkey!" yelled Python. "Did you eat my eggs?"

"What?" Monkey said, swinging towards her.

"I said why did you steal my eggs?"

Monkey jumped down with a thud. "I did not steal your eggs!" he said angrily. "You know I only like bananas!"

What should poor Python do now? She'd have no friends left in the jungle if she kept thinking they stole her eggs.

Just before sunrise, Python slithered to the other side of the jungle, hoping to start afresh. Within a few minutes she found a nice place behind some thick plants, and once again laid her eggs. Then she went to find something to eat. She was starving.

Just as Python was turning the corner, a pregnant woman from the village came along, carrying a bucket of water. She too was very hungry.

"I hope I find something to eat in the jungle today," she said to herself, looking all around.

For several months the pregnant woman had

been finding eggs in a cornfield, behind a palm tree and in the middle of banana trees. She didn't know who owned the eggs, but they were very delicious indeed.

A few minutes later, the woman found white roundish shapes lying on some thick plants and moved a bit closer to inspect the objects.

"Oh, how lucky am I!" she cried as she saw that they were eggs. In fact, there were six eggs in all. She picked them all up and carefully put them in her bag, before hurrying home to cook them.

Shortly afterwards Python came back and found that her eggs had gone yet again. This time she vowed to catch the selfish thief. In order to do this, she decided she was going to try something different.

She began to sing a song. It was a very sad song. At first she sang quietly, then she sang loudly...

Akwaeke oli ma, akwaeke oli ma!
(Python's eggs! Python's eggs!)
Dooli ma ma! Dooli ma!
Akwaeke mu debelu eba ofukwa!
(The python's eggs I left here are missing!)
Dooli ma ma! Dooli ma!

By now the woman was about to open her front door. She heard the song and paused. At once she knew the song was about the eggs she'd stolen, and she also knew they belonged to a python. But she wasn't going to give them back. So she said to herself, 'What can a snake do to me? After all, she's just a snake.'

She went into her kitchen, and lit a fire. Then she boiled all the eggs. She was looking forward to having a huge lunch.

When the eggs were cooked, she peeled them one by one very carefully. Then she picked up an egg. She was about to shove it into her opened mouth, when she heard the same sad song again.

She got really angry. 'You silly snake, what can you do to me? You're just a snake,' she said to herself.

Then she shoved the egg into her mouth, and began to chew it. The egg tasted very delicious indeed.

Meanwhile, Python carried on singing her sad song. She was heartbroken. But it didn't stop the woman shoving one more egg into her mouth, and within minutes she'd eaten the whole lot!

The woman sat on a chair and relaxed. She didn't care about Python or her sad song.

Then, a few minutes later, something happened. The woman began to have a stomach pain. 'Oh, why am I in so much pain?' she said to herself as she twisted this way and that. But the pain didn't stop - it was as if her belly was on fire.

"Oh my poor belly!" she cried.

Just then, she heard another song. It wasn't an angry song, but a song that was sung in sympathy. Python sang,

Nwanyị ime ndo, ndo, ndo, ndo, ndo!
(Pregnant woman, I'm sorry!)
Nwanyị ime ndo, ndo, ndo, ndo, ndo!

As she listened to the song the woman began to feel very guilty. 'Oh no, what have I done to this poor snake?' she said to herself. 'I should never have eaten her eggs. Now she has nothing. I'm so sorry!'

She got up and went outside, and shouted at the top of her voice, "Please forgive me, Snake, I'm so sorry. I'll never eat your eggs again!"

Gradually her belly stopped hurting her, and from that day onwards the woman never ate Python's eggs again.

And what about Python? Well, she soon laid more eggs and this time they hatched successfully.

The moral of this story is - don't take what doesn't belong to you.

Talented Grasshopper

Many years ago Grasshopper made the best cooking oil in the jungle. It was very tasty, light, smooth and pure. And it was a lovely yellow colour, just like an egg yolk.

All the other animals, even Lion, made oils that tasted and smelt horrible. Was it any wonder their food tasted pretty bad?

Once poor Lion added so much salt to his oil, he couldn't eat his food! So next time he cooked, he swapped the salt for red hot chillies. But they were so hot they made his eyes water and his nose run - and still his food tasted bad. In the end he began to skip his meals. He even stopped eating his favourite snack, plantain chips. He just couldn't stand the smell or taste any more, because of the bad-tasting oil!

Pushing his plate aside one day, Lion said to himself, 'There must be something I can do to make my food taste better.' He began to think, but it's very hard to concentrate if your mouth tastes like rotten eggs mixed with lemon! Still, he didn't give up, and at last he had an idea.

'Why don't I organise an oil tasting festival? Everyone loves festivals, and that way I can find out who makes the best oil in the jungle, and get some for myself!'

The next day Lion called a meeting, and all the animals came.

Lion stood up. "I'd like to tell you about a new

festival and..."

But he was quickly interrupted by the excited animals. They couldn't wait to have a great time. They were already discussing all the things they were going to do when they got to the festival.

"Quiet, everyone," roared Lion, and then he explained a bit more about the new festival. He added, "Whoever has the best tasting oil will be presented with the key to a beautiful house, built by the best architects and builders in the jungle!"

The animals exploded into loud cheers. They danced, did back-flips and sang. In fact the entire jungle shook with joy!

Lion set the festival for two weeks' time, to give the animals time to prepare their oils.

As soon as the meeting ended, some of the animals began discussing the big prize. Who wouldn't want a new house built by the best architects and builders in the jungle?

"I want a new burrow," said Rabbit to Grasshopper. "My old one is letting in water."

"Me too!" said Grasshopper, remembering his windowless house. He could never see the grass or the trees from his home.

All the animals rushed back to their various

homes to start making their oils. Each day was spent mixing, blending and tasting the oils. Some added herbs to their existing oils, others chilli peppers, to give them extra spice and flavour.

Not to be outdone by the others, Tortoise poured his old oils into a clay pot to give them a distinctive flavour.

Grasshopper, on the other hand, did what he always did. He made his oil with great care and dedication, and of course with his wife's encouragement. His wife, Anekwu, always sang a beautiful song for her husband while he made the oil; she'd call him by his name as she sang. Grasshopper's name was Ụrira.

So Grasshopper perched at the edge of a frying pan, and beat his wings furiously while his wife sang,

Ụrira di Anekwu, Ụrira,
(Ụrira the husband of Anekwu,)
Ụrira di Anekwu, Ụrira,
Eju aghụlụ okụ, Ụrira.
(The frying pan is hot, Ụrira.)

Soon, rich golden oil flowed out of his wings

into the hot pan. The heat from the pan made it easier for the oil to pour out. And it flowed and flowed. When the pan was full of oil, his wife stopped singing and Grasshopper flew down.

***

On the day of the festival most of the animals poured their oils into beautiful handmade jars, to impress Lion. Grasshopper, on the other hand, put his into a very simple jar.

With the oils corked and sealed in different containers, the animals gently carried them to the king's palace.

Tables and chairs were already laid out by the time they got there. The whole place had been decorated, too. There were colourful banners hanging from poles and there was music as well.

After they had all settled down, Lion declared the festival open. Then he called the animals one by one to present their oils for tasting.

The first oil he tasted was horrible! It was heavy and nasty and it smelt like an old blanket. He quickly spat it out. Then he tried the second one, which smelt like a pair of trainers worn by a giant with dirty feet. He spat that out, too.

Bravely, Lion carried on tasting the oils, although he was beginning to feel sick from all the nasty smells and tastes. He was just about to give up, when Grasshopper begged him to try his.

Reluctantly Lion raised a spoonful of oil to his mouth, and a lovely aroma floated up to his nostrils. He thought he was in heaven, it smelt so delicious. Pausing for a few seconds to absorb the sweet smell, Lion then licked the spoon. The oil was as rich and smooth as honey!

"This is brilliant, Grasshopper! Does it taste good in plantain chips?" asked Lion.

"Yes, sir, it does! In fact it's great in all the dishes!"

Lion was very pleased indeed. At last he was

going to eat his favourite snack. He presented Grasshopper with the first prize, and the keys to a new house. Then he took some of the oil home.

Most of the animals were very happy for Grasshopper. They all congratulated him on making the best tasting oil in the jungle.

The next day they gathered in small groups under the trees, or around the riverbanks where they went to drink, to talk about Grasshopper.

Soon he became a celebrity. It was incredible, unbelievable! As with all celebrities, there was lots of gossip about what he had for dinner every night, and who was going to be his best friend. The animals argued over whose house he was going to visit next.

They followed Grasshopper wherever he went. Sometimes they stood around for ages patiently waiting to catch a glimpse of him, just like fans do for film stars. Even Lion called the grasshopper a hero, and invited him to all his parties.

But there was one animal who was not so impressed by Grasshopper's fame, and that was Tortoise.

"I don't see why he should get all this attention," Tortoise complained. He began to get very jealous of Grasshopper, and the more he thought about him the angrier he got.

When Tortoise heard that Lion was running out of oil, he thought to himself: "Here's my chance to show him that I can make delicious oil too!"

But could he really make delicious oil, and how could he do it? Tortoise thought and thought, and at last he came up with a plan.

He said to his wife, "Let's move right next door to Grasshopper!"

His wife, whose name was Aniga, was baffled by this, but she agreed to move house.

Now Tortoise was able to keep an eye on his new neighbour 24 hours a day! Within hours of moving in, he saw Grasshopper perched on the edge of a frying pan while his wife sang a song to him. And what's more, oil was pouring out of his wings like water!

Tortoise was excited. 'I'm bigger than him,' he said to himself. 'Imagine the amount of oil I can make when my wife sings to me. Of course she'll have to call out my name!'

At once he rushed off to the market to buy a gigantic frying pan. When he came back, he taught his wife how to sing the oil song, and insisted she called out his name while she sang.

As soon as she'd learnt the song, Tortoise asked her to light a fire, and when it was lit, he placed the frying pan on top and climbed in. Then he asked his wife to sing the song with all her heart.

As soon as she began to sing, Tortoise began to dance frantically. She sang,

> Mbe di Aniga Mbe,
> (Tortoise, the husband of Aniga,)
> Mbe di Aniga Mbe,
> Eju aghụlụ okụ, Mbe,
> (The frying pan is hot now, Tortoise,)
> Mbe di Ani ga Mbe.

And Tortoise stamped and stumbled about in the pan. While this was going on, the frying pan was getting dangerously hot - it had been on the fire for some minutes. But Tortoise was so busy thinking about how rich and famous he was going to be, he didn't notice how hot he was getting.

All this time no oil had poured out of his shell. In fact it was as dry as a stone! Still Tortoise kept on dancing, trying to make the oil flow. Meanwhile the pan was getting hotter and hotter.

At last Tortoise could bear the heat no longer. "Help, help!" he cried. "Someone help me, please!"

He could feel his tail beginning to burn, and he called out again.

Soon his neighbours, including Grasshopper, rushed to help him. They pulled him out of the hot pan just in time, before he was too badly burned.

Later, Grasshopper applied some of his oil on Tortoise's tail. It was wonderfully soothing.

Tortoise was ashamed of his foolish behaviour. "From now on, I won't copy anyone else," he said to his wife. "I'll be myself and concentrate on my own talents."

And did Tortoise learn from his mistakes? Maybe, but only time will tell!

The moral of this story is - jealousy does no one any good.

Why the Lizard Nods his Head

There was once a lizard who loved sunbathing. He'd drop whatever he was doing the minute the sun came out, and rush to his favourite rock. There he'd lie for hours and hours.

As you might have guessed by now, Lizard didn't like working. In fact, he hated it! He used to say, "What's the point of running around when you can relax in the sun and enjoy life?"

Instead he devoted his time to telling stories, eating, and admiring his own reflection in the water. He'd say, "Look how handsome I am!" to anyone who would listen.

Indeed, he was handsome. From his chest all the way down to his tail he was light green, but his neck and head were the colour of a ripe tomato. He really stood out in a crowd.

The other things that made Lizard stand out were his stories. They were funny, exciting and entertaining. Animals would cram into his tiny front room to listen to him. Usually, he began telling stories at sunset and carried on until darkness covered everything like a huge blanket. His voice would rise and fall like the waves in the sea, as he enchanted his audience.

Soon the animals began to offer him food in exchange for his stories, and before long he was getting dinner and breakfast, too!

As Lizard got more and more food he became more and more choosy about what he ate. In the end he ate only the most delicious meals and threw away the rest.

One night, just after he'd finished telling stories, Tortoise approached him and said, "You've never eaten my food before, have you?"

"I don't think so," replied Lizard coolly. He'd had so much to eat, he didn't want any more that night.

"Well, try this," said Tortoise, and he held out a plate of *egusi* (melon seed) stew.

Lizard took it reluctantly, but when the aroma of the food floated into his nostrils, he changed his mind. He quickly ate the whole lot. He even licked the plate clean!

After that, he and Tortoise became great friends. He ate all his meals at Tortoise's house. He was like a celebrity with his own personal chef!

One day Tortoise heard there was to be a competition for the best chef in the jungle, and he decided to enter it. He chose to make Okra Stew with Pounded Yams. Okra are green vegetables shaped like fingers, and when cooked with palm oil they are very delicious.

So Tortoise went to the market and bought the finest ingredients for his stew. He came home and cooked it, then went off to work, planning to take the food to the judging tent later.

Soon after Tortoise left, Lizard dropped by to say hello. But when he realized Tortoise was out, he decided he'd wait for his friend to come home.

After a while, feeling rather hungry, he said to himself, 'I'm sure Tortoise has some food in his house, he's always cooking.' He went up to the door and found that Tortoise had forgotten to lock up before leaving for work.

Lizard went into the house and began looking for food. Within seconds he found a tray on top of a cupboard, and on the tray stood a bowl of okra stew and a plate piled high with pounded yam.

He had a little taste. The food was scrumptious! So he ate a little more and then a little more, saying to himself, 'This is delicious!'

Soon he'd eaten the lot!

With his stomach bursting, Lizard belched loudly and staggered outside. He just made it to his favourite rock, before falling asleep.

When Tortoise came home, he couldn't believe his eyes! His house was in a terrible mess, and worst of all, someone had eaten all his okra stew.

"Who could have done this?" he cried.

His neighbour, Snake, heard him wailing, and came to see what had happened. "What's the matter, my friend?" he said.

"Someone has eaten my okra stew. I was going to take it to the competition this evening," sobbed Tortoise.

"Don't cry," said Snake, "there will be other competitions."

And he was right. A few weeks later there was another cookery competition. This time Tortoise chose to prepare egusi stew cooked in palm oil, and served with pounded yam.

When he'd finished cooking, he said, "I'll take the food to the judging tent after work." But this time Tortoise didn't take any chances. He locked the door before leaving.

Once more, Lizard dropped by. As he waited for his friend to come home, he felt hungry again. He remembered the delicious meal he'd eaten before, and headed for Tortoise's door. It was locked. So he went round the back and saw that a window had been left half open. He climbed in quickly.

Lizard went straight to the kitchen and found two dishes containing egusi stew and pounded yam on the table. He took off the lids and dived in at once. The flavour of the egusi stew spread across his tongue, and it was delicious! He ate and ate, munching away as if there was no tomorrow.

"This time, my friend, you've surpassed yourself!" he said, and when he'd finished every scrap of stew he went off to lie in the sun.

Hours later, Tortoise came home and found that someone had eaten his food again. How he cried! He wailed and wailed.

His neighbour Snake rushed out once more. "What's the matter?" he asked.

"Someone has eaten the food I cooked for the competition AGAIN!" sobbed Tortoise.

"You can't go on like this," said Snake decisively. "You must set a trap! That way you can catch the thief. "

Hearing this, Tortoise brightened up a little, and started to work out a plan.

***

A few weeks later there was a third competition, and Tortoise had another chance to show off his cooking skills.

For this competition he chose *ogbono* stew cooked in palm oil and served with pounded yam. Eating *ogboño* stew is like eating a tasty marshmallow, except that it's savoury not sweet.

Anyway, Tortoise cooked it well and then he set his trap. The trap was some tiny pieces of sharp sticks, which he tied together into a bundle. He buried the bundle deep inside the stew so that the thief wouldn't see it. Then he left the food on the kitchen table, and went off to work.

As usual Lizard came to visit his friend, and when he discovered that Tortoise wasn't in he was relieved. "I shall have a lovely lunch again," he said to himself as he headed for the back of the house.

This time the window was wide open, and Lizard was overjoyed. 'Tortoise, my friend,' he said to himself, 'you're getting rather forgetful, leaving your window open like this!'

He went straight in. On the kitchen table stood two huge dishes, one containing *ogboño* stew and the other, pounded yam. Lizard's mouth began to water. He whisked off the lids and began to eat the delicious food at once.

He ate and ate until his belly was almost bursting. Finally, he got to the last little bit of food at the bottom of the plate and decided to swallow it whole. He scooped up the food and stuffed it into his mouth. But just as he was about to swallow it, he felt a sharp pain. Oh, it was dreadful. Something was stuck in his throat!

Lizard coughed and stamped about, but nothing worked. By now his throat was on fire, and no matter how hard he tried he couldn't get rid of the pain. Coughing loudly, and shaking his head up and down, he staggered outside to get some help.

It was then that Snake heard him, and rushed out to see what was going on. As soon as he saw what had happened he raised the alarm.

"Thief! Thief! Everyone, come and see the thief!" he cried.

Lizard tried to escape, but it was too late. All the animals came so fast he had no time to run away. Soon a big crowd had gathered in front of Tortoise's house.

"What were you doing in Tortoise's house?" asked one of the animals.

"Me, in Tortoise's house, never!" said Lizard, coughing and spluttering.

At last Tortoise himself appeared. "So it's you who's been eating my food!" he said sadly. "And I thought you were my friend."

Lizard was so ashamed he just ran away.

And to this day, Lizard is trying to dislodge the sticks in his throat, and he still nods his head up and down, up and down.

The moral of this story is - don't be greedy!

The Wrestler
and the Ghost

There was once a very special man, who stood head
and shoulders above everyone in his village. He
was exceptionally strong, agile and fast. He could
smash chairs in half with his bare hands or run as
fast as a gazelle, and yet he never felt tired!

What's more, the man was a wrestler, probably
the best in the world. He won all his matches with
ease. People came from far and wide just to set
eyes on him. The man's name was Ojadili...

When Ojadili was a baby he was tiny and frail.
The villagers advised his mother to wrap him up
in banana leaves to keep him warm. In those days
banana leaves, which are gigantic, were used as

incubators because they retain heat. So baby Ojadili was wrapped like a parcel, and afterwards he grew into a strong boy.

When he was six years old he could lift metal buckets filled with water. His family was amazed.

By the time he was ten years old he was lifting weights meant for grown men! It was incredible.

One day his uncle saw him carrying huge slabs of stones as if they were made out of papier-mâché. He was so impressed by his young nephew's strength that he taught him to wrestle. Ojadili was a great student and soon he'd learnt all his uncle could teach him.

In the meantime, he carried on growing. He grew and grew until he was taller than everyone else. His friends called him an iroko tree, because it is the tallest tree in the village and the strongest, too.

When Ojadili was sixteen years old he won his first real wrestling match and he went on to win many more matches.

His fame grew rapidly, spreading beyond his village to neighbouring towns and cities!

Soon, everybody was showering Ojadili with gifts - money, jewellery and land. Parents named their children after him, hoping they'd grow up as strong as the great wrestler. Singers and musicians sang beautiful songs in his honour. Storytellers wove countless exciting tales about his strength. Even hairdressers named hair styles after him. It was as if everyone had caught Ojadili-fever.

Yet Ojadili wasn't satisfied with these

achievements. He wanted more and more fame. Perhaps if the moon and the stars were to bow down before him he might at last be happy.

One day he said to his friends, "Think how famous I'd be if, in my next wrestling match, I challenged a ghost and won."

His friends were horrified. The mere mention of a ghost caused the hairs at the back of their necks to prickle, and a chill to run down their spines. What was Ojadili thinking of? Had he gone mad?

Finally, one of his friends plucked up courage and said to the great wrestler, "It's very dangerous to challenge a ghost to a wrestling match. Please don't do it."

"That's right," said another, trembling like a leaf. "We beg you not to!"

But Ojadili just thought, 'Why should I listen to a bunch of cowards with spines as weak as rotten fruit?'

And so it was that a few days later the famous wrestler went out looking for a ghost. Every night for seven weeks, he trekked for hours in dense forests, caves, river banks, and even old graveyards, But he never found any ghosts.

Then, one night, when Ojadili had almost given

up, there was a knock on his door. He hesitated. Could this be a ghost?

He went to the door. There, standing a few inches in front of him, was a tiny old man with big eyes.

Ojadili was puzzled. "What do you want?" he asked sharply.

"I am here to make your wishes come true," said the old man in a trembling voice.

"My wishes?" said Ojadili, laughing. How could this old man possibly be a wrestler?

The old man quickly reassured him. "I'm not a wrestler," he said. "I'm just a messenger."

"OK, what's your message then?" said Ojadili rudely.

"The strongest ghost wishes to challenge you to a wrestling match," replied the old man.

"Well, come in. Come in!" Ojadili yelled in excitement, pulling the old man into his house.

So the old man, who was carrying a tattered old bag on his left shoulder, explained that he'd come from the land of the spirits, where all the ghosts lived.

"Young man," he said, "have you ever wrestled a ghost before?"

"No, why?" replied the wrestler, feeling a little irritated.

"Do you know what the risks are?" persisted the old man.

But Ojadili just ignored him, and went off to pack his travelling bag. He came back a few minutes later with everything he needed: clothes, a chewing stick for cleaning teeth, in case he had to stay the night, some money and some food.

When the old man saw that Ojadili was determined to go ahead with the match, he said, "Let me show you how to get to the land of the spirits."

He slid the tattered bag off his shoulder, and took out several leaves. He rubbed these on the palms of his hands until some juice came out.

"Now," said the old man, looking up at Ojadili, "I want you to squeeze this juice into your eyes. It will transport you to the land of the spirits, and it will also help you to see ghosts."

Ojadili couldn't wait. He snatched the mushy leaves from his visitor and squeezed them hard....

***

All of a sudden, Ojadili found himself in a strange land. It was a desolate place, miserable and grey. There were no shops, trees or flowers - in fact there was nothing at all.

Undeterred, Ojadili began searching for the wrestler ghost. He crossed countless rivers, hills and deserts, and the only noise he could hear was the crunching sound of his feet on the dry, cracked ground.

Eventually he came across a skinny little man. His skin was dusty grey, just like the colour of the soil. His arms were like knitting pins and his head was the size of an orange.

"Welcome to the land of the spirits!" said the little man, smiling.

But Ojadili had no time for pleasantries. "Take me to the strongest ghost in your land!" he said impatiently.

"I am the strongest ghost!" was the reply.

Ojadili threw back his head and laughed. He hadn't come all this way to wrestle this weak little man. Besides, how could he be a ghost? Surely ghosts didn't have bodies or wear clothes?

But the ghost already knew what Ojadili was thinking. "Oh yes, we can have bodies just like you," he said. "We borrow them from earth all the time."

And now, for the first time in his life, Ojadili was a little scared.

There was indeed something odd about the ghost. Could he have borrowed his eyes from someone much bigger than him? For they were as round as bottle tops, set deep inside a small face, and as for those ears of his, surely they must have belonged to a cat. They were covered in fur, and were very pointy and small.

The ghost's appearance was the least of Ojadili's problems, because all of a sudden he puffed out his thin chest and took a step toward him. Was he about to challenge him to a match?

Ojadili quickly dropped his bag on the ground, and flexed his muscles.

The ghost flexed his muscles too.

Ojadili kept his eye on him for a few seconds before he made his move. Then he grabbed the ghost by the arm and tried to trip him up.

But the ghost was as solid as a wall - he didn't move at all.

Ojadili tried again and again, but it was useless. He had to admit the ghost was just too strong for him!

A few minutes later, when Ojadili was completely worn out, the ghost saw his chance. He stepped forward and grabbed Ojadili by the arm. If he could throw him down on the ground, he'd win the match.

Luckily, Ojadili was like a piece of soap and he slipped quickly from the ghost's grip. Now it was his chance to win the match once and for all.

He summoned all his strength and grabbed the ghost again, and this time he moved very fast. He lifted him right off the ground and then dropped him with all his strength. The ghost landed on his back, and didn't get up.

The match was over.

The great wrestler had won again - or had he?

As Ojadili turned to leave, the ghost scratched him on his back, and gave him a deep wound that ran all the way from his neck down to his tail bone.

The pain was unbearable. Ojadili screamed and began to run. All he wanted was to get home as quickly as possible.

Ghosts of all shapes and sizes heard his screams and crawled out of holes in the ground, some from underneath rocks and stones, others from the body of the fallen ghost. They all gave chase, but Ojadili was too fast for them.

Ghosts never give up, however, and they vowed to find Ojadili. To this day, they're still looking for him - roaming all over the earth, searching for the great wrestler!

The moral of this story is - be happy with your talents and use them well.

Photograph by Emeka Malbert

Ifeoma Onyefulu was brought up in a traditional village in Eastern Nigeria. After completing a business management course, she trained as a photographer, contributing to a number of magazines and exhibiting widely. Ifeoma's highly acclaimed children's books are renowned for countering negative images of Africa by celebrating both its traditional village life and its urban life. *A is for Africa*, her first book for Frances Lincoln, has become a classic title in the genre of cultural diversity. Ifeoma has twice won the Children's Africana Book Award: Best Book for Young Children in the USA. *Here Comes our Bride* won the award in 2005, and *Ikenna Goes to Nigeria* in 2008. Her latest picture books, launching the First Experiences series, are for preschool children: *Deron Goes to Nursery School* and *Grandma Comes to Stay*. Ifeoma lives in London with her two sons.

To find out more about Ifeoma visit her website:
www.ifeomaonyefulu.co.uk

Complete list of books for children by Ifeoma Onyefulu

First Concepts

A is for Africa
Chidi Only Likes Blue
Emeka's Gift
A Triangle for Adaora

Celebrating Nigerian Culture

Ebele's Favourite
My Grandfather is a Magician
One Big Family

Celebrating Special Occasions

An African Christmas
Here Comes our Bride!
Saying Goodbye
Welcome, Dede!

A Child Returns to his Roots

Ikenna Goes to Nigeria

First Experiences

Deron Goes to Nursery School
Grandma Comes to Stay